THE
OXBOY

BY
ANNE
MAZER

ALFRED A. KNOPF, PUBLISHER
NEW YORK

TO PHIL, DEBBIE, TOSHI, RAKA, AND SAM

THIS IS A BORZOI BOOK PUBLISHED BY ALFRED A. KNOPF, INC.

Text copyright © 1993 by Anne Mazer
Jacket illustration © 1993 by Stasys Eidrigevičius

Library of Congress Cataloging-in-Publication Data

Mazer, Anne.
The Oxboy / by Anne Mazer.
p.   cm.
Summary: A young boy who is half-human and half-ox struggles to survive in a society where animals are hated and contact with them is prohibited.
ISBN 0-679-84191-1
[1. Prejudices—Fiction. 2.Human–animal relationships—Fiction.]
I. Title.
PZ7.M473960x   1993   [Fic]—dc20   93-37199

Manufactured in the United States of America
10 9 8 7 6 5 4 3 2 1

CONTENTS

MY FATHER

No one can tell that I am the son of an ox. Like my father, I am hardworking, and I have a stubborn, tenacious nature. But so do many pure humans. Like any farm boy bred in the open air, I have broad shoulders and brown skin. Some call me ugly. I have a wide nose with flaring nostrils and a low forehead over which coarse brown hair falls in thick clumps. My toenails and fingernails are extremely hard. My eyes, however, are delicate and almond-shaped—an inheritance from my tall and graceful mother that sits oddly on my blunt features.

My mother has no close friends, and I have never met her relations. I may have grandparents, cousins, and aunts, as other children, but I have not so much as heard their names. My mother cut all connection with her family when she and my father ran away together.

I have not forgotten my father, though he left when I was five. He was never a father like all the others; kinder, perhaps. Together we roamed through the fields for hours, and from his back I used to reach for the hanging pear or the high, ripe berry. Sometimes my mother would join us, and then we wore crowns of daisies that she wove for us.

When my father wanted to rest, he would drop to the ground and put his head in my mother's lap. His powerful muscles tensed and then relaxed. And she would comb his long coarse hair until his eyes closed and he drifted off to sleep. Then my mother too would fall asleep, while I searched the ground for my father's hairs. I lined my pockets with great handfuls of them; they made a soft bed for the insects I liked to play with.

Each year my father left us for a short time to join his brothers and sisters, the intelligent animals of the forest. They hid from men, and even from certain animals, and were so difficult to find that my father sometimes came home without catching a glimpse of them. The year I was five he returned tired and thin but glowing with happiness. A blue velvet sack hung from his neck. Inside were a handful of pearly stones he had brought back for me. He promised that he would take me with him on his next journey into the forest.

When my father was away, my mother would always tell me the story of how she met him. How she had wandered far from home and found herself in a strange meadow. She was searching for a path or stream to follow when a great brown ox came out of the forest.

She trembled in fear, but then the ox spoke to her.

"My lady, do not be afraid." His voice was soft and deep. "I will not hurt you."

Like all children, my mother had learned in school that oxen were degraded beasts of burden whose sole purpose was to toil in the fields for men. The few such animals she had known were miserable starved creatures, gelded, with long welts along their hides, who drank foul water and ate moldy hay. But this ox was a splendid creature. Its muscles surged under its glossy coat; its eyes were bright yet gentle. She had never seen an animal like that, an animal that could be called beautiful.

The ox told her to climb onto his back, and she obeyed. Then he carried her swiftly home. He let her off where no one would see him, then vanished into the forest.

When she got home, she could not stop thinking of the ox.

"I went to find him the next week," said my mother, "though if I had been discovered, we both would have been killed.

"We became closer and closer. One day I went to see him and never went home. We roamed for a long time through pathless forests, meeting the hidden animals, both intelligent and dumb. Then we came here with you . . ."

The cottage where my mother, my father, and I lived was like a sweet-smelling barn. It was far off the main road, at the end of a tumbled path overgrown with clover and blackberries. Stacked in the living room were bales of prickly hay that I could climb on or hide behind. My mother made a bed of straw for my father in their room, where he sometimes slept. In the morning he came to the table, where she set a dish of fresh water for him. She scattered hay for grazing over our floor—our house always smelled fresh and clean. At night when he wanted to come in from the fields, my father poked his head through the window and my mother opened wide the kitchen door for him.

Sometimes my father stayed in the barn. In the morning I would leap from my bed and run to the barn, where I would fling open the doors. Then I would climb the long ropes that hung from the rafters and swing over the bales of hay. My father would pretend to be sleeping, and I would land right on his back. Then with a great cry he would clamber to his feet, stamp out the door, and gallop around and around the yard while I screamed with joy.

And so I lived for the first five years of my life.

THE PRINCE
AND THE CAT

Often at night, after we had finished our supper, my father stretched out on the living room floor while my mother wound spools of brightly colored yarn that she wove into blankets for my father and me. Sometimes my father asked for a story. I leaned against his warm flanks. My mother put down the yarn. Then she began.

"In the beginning of time, animals and humans lived separately, and neither thought to intrude on the other's world. They caught glimpses of each other when animals strayed to the towns or men and women wandered too far in the forests, but both were mysterious to the other.

"A prince was born. It was foretold that he would dream of animals, and as a young boy he often dreamed of a majestic gray cat who spoke to him. The prince was an unusual student, and by the time he was twenty-one he spoke and read eight hundred languages.

"The hall where the prince held court was often filled with scores of visitors all speaking at once, none in the same tongue. To go to his hall, some said, was like being at the ocean—many separate voices blending into one unfathomable wave. Only the prince could distinguish the individual strands in the roar of language.

"One day while the prince was walking in a meadow a cat appeared and began to follow him.

"The cat was gray and large, with pale blue eyes that watched the prince constantly. The cat went home with the prince that night, and the prince invited the cat first to his table, where he fed him with his own hand from a milk-white dish, and then to his chamber, where he made a bed for him on a heap of cushions.

"Soon the cat and the prince were inseparable companions.

"When the prince bathed in the river, the great cat slept on the bank. When the prince sat in his library and pored over his books written in all the languages of the world, the cat peered over his shoulder as though he too were reading every word.

"During the audiences the prince held in his hall, the cat, tail twitching and blue eyes gazing steadily, lay at the prince's feet as if sitting in judgment over all the lords, ladies, and simple people of the land.

"One day while the prince was holding court, the cat rose and began to speak. 'My gracious lord,' he said. 'Now is the time.'

"The prince ordered the hall emptied.

"The prince and the cat stayed together in the hall thirty days and thirty nights. No one was allowed to enter except to bring food, drink, or bedding. The men and women of the court gathered outside the door, straining to hear their prince's voice. But all they heard was a faint or sometimes louder mewing, and then silence.

"When the prince and the cat emerged, the prince announced that he had learned the language of cats.

" 'This cat knows many things which

men and women cannot apprehend through their five senses. He has a wisdom equal to, or greater than, mine.'

" 'The cat tells me that each species has its healing lore, its wisdom and knowledge. Some animals have found the secret of peace and contentment.'

"Then the prince declared that he was leaving for the forest. 'For I would make the acquaintance of the many animals there, in order to learn their language and teach them ours, and to gain help for humankind.'

"Soon after, the prince disappeared, leaving the cat to rule and counsel in his place. For the cat was a king among his own kind, and well-equipped to rule.

"The prince roamed in the wild as both student and teacher. The gray cat fell in love with a musical lady of the court who played the harp and flute, and they were married the next spring, when the prince returned. The wedding was held in a large field and was attended by men, women, bears, wolves, foxes, leopards, cats, and lions.

"At the feast that followed, the prince announced that as a wedding gift, he was leaving his kingdom in trust to the cat and his bride, while he would continue to search out the many animals of the forest.

"The gray cat and his lady bride ruled wisely and well, as did their five sons after them—tall and dashing feline princes with pale blue eyes, pointed claws, and up-turned whiskers.

"That was the First Wedding. From that time on, humans and other animals began to marry."

My father always sighed contentedly at

the end of this story. And later I climbed between the cool sheets of my bed and listened to the howls, squeals, and roars that came from the forest every night. Sometimes I was afraid of these strange noises, but after my mother would tell us this story, I would hear them as the calls of my brothers and sisters.

WE ARE BETRAYED

One day my father and I were plowing the garden together. The earth was wet and resisted the plow, but my father was strong. Although it was a misty spring day, the sun burned through the clouds, and soon I had to take off my jacket and pour a bucket of water over my father's back to cool him.

We were breaking new ground, and I was tossing rocks aside, when my father halted. Even at five years of age I knew how unusual it was for him to stop in the middle of work.

I jiggled the harness, but he didn't budge. "Father?"

I turned then and saw my mother. She was running toward us, her dress muddied, her hands empty. In spite of the heat of the day and her exertion, her face was white as a stone. Behind her a bedsheet floated from a clothesline, and flock of north-flying geese circled overhead.

She came to a halt a few feet away from us. "You must go," she called to my father.

My father moved toward her, and she held up her hand to stop him. "They are coming," my mother said. "We are betrayed. The hunters are coming."

They had forgotten about me, standing by the plow.

"I saw them at the market," my mother said. "I came as fast as I could. They bragged about the bounty you would bring them."

"Are you sure?" my father asked. "Were they not speaking of another?"

"They spoke of a bull living outside the town with a young woman and a boy."

The wind picked up and the sun went behind a cloud, and I was suddenly cold and wanted to be inside our cottage in front of a fire and playing with the pearly stones my father had brought me not too long ago.

"Who has betrayed us?" my father asked.

"Louk," said my mother.

The beggar's skinny crooked face with its fierce eyes rose up before me. My mother had given him cakes and bread when she saw him at the market. Once, during a snowstorm, he had knocked on our door. Luckily my father was in the barn, but I had seen Louk staring suspiciously at the bales of hay in our living room.

In the morning my mother had gone to the barn to bring my father fresh hay and water.

"Why do you feed that bull before yourself?" Louk had asked when she came back.

It was the first time I had heard my father referred to as a bull, and in Louk's mouth the word had a menacing sound.

"Oh, I am not hungry," my mother said.

"The boy has not eaten either."

I was young and did not understand. I snatched a handful of hay from behind the couch and stuffed it into my mouth. "Here is my breakfast!" I announced.

Louk's dark eyes glittered. "Ah . . ."

"Take that out of your mouth!" my mother ordered in a voice I had never heard before. "Are you a human boy or an animal?"

Her words confused me, and I began to cry.

My mother ignored my tears. Instead she turned to Louk. "You must be hungry. I have many good things for you. Come, seat yourself at our table."

"Louk sold us for a bounty," my mother now said to my father. "Go. Go!"

"I will not leave you," said my father, but my mother had already sprung forward and was freeing him from his harness.

"You must go—and quickly."

My father shook his head.

"They will kill the boy." She whispered this. "They will kill all of us if they find you here."

Only then did my father bow his head. He turned to me one last time and nuzzled my cheek with his soft cool nose, then disappeared into the forest.

THE BLUE HUNTERS

In the cottage my mother took out a bucket and a mop and began to clean. I leaned out the window as though my father might be there by the barn, waiting for me to run out and jump on his back. But the barn and yard were empty.

My mother carried the bales of hay stacked behind the couch out to the barn. She flung open the windows, washed the bedding, and scrubbed floors, ceilings, closets, and shelves. She went from room to room plucking stray hairs and bits of straw from carpets and chairs, sweeping all the long coarse brown hairs into a pile which she burned in the fireplace. Then she made me empty my pockets into the fireplace too.

When she had finished with the house, she took me outside, where we shoveled piles of dung and spread it in the garden my father had plowed. Then we planted squash and watermelon and pumpkins and tomatoes.

When my mother had eradicated every trace of my father from the house and the yard, she sat on the couch and stared at the empty wall. I played near her, hiding behind the couch and building towers with my pearly stones.

The hunters did not come that day. They did not come the next day. Or the day after.

★   ★   ★

When they knocked at our door, it was I who opened it.

One man stepped forward. He was a local farmer, a friendly man, large and jovial, who had given me a whistle once when I had gone to market with my mother and who always complimented us on our fine produce.

But today he had a rifle slung over his shoulder, wore a long red jacket, and his face—like the others' faces—was painted blue. I fled behind the couch.

My mother rose and spoke in the manner of our country. "What may I give you this day?"

"We are looking for your husband," said the man. His face shone blue and cruel like the moon, and I retreated farther behind the couch.

"My husband is dead."

"Who is the child's father?"

"I told you he was dead."

The man walked over to the fireplace, where he picked up an iron shovel and turned over the ashes. Another one of the blue hunters opened cupboards and took out cups and saucers, plates and napkins. He ran his fingers over the bare shelves, peered inside empty milk pitchers, tapped walls.

"I do not know what you search for," said my mother. "We have nothing, my son and I."

The hunters did not answer. Two of them went into the bedroom. When they came out, one man was holding a single stalk of hay, which he twirled thoughtfully between his thumb and his forefinger.

They asked to see our papers.

From a small drawer in the kitchen table my mother brought out some documents, shiny silver pieces of paper that gleamed as she walked across the room.

The leader scanned the papers quickly. "My apologies, lady."

Then he looked at me. I had come out from behind the couch and was hanging on to my mother's leg.

"Where are his papers?" he asked.

"The child's papers were burned in a fire," my mother said. "I am sending away for new ones. They haven't arrived yet."

The man stared at both of us for a long moment.

He adjusted the rifle on his shoulder. "You had better get him a father fast."

The blue hunters tramped out the door. They didn't bother to shut it behind them.

A few days later we left our house, our

beds, our table and warm fireplace, and the garden we had so carefully tended. Taking only a few belongings that could fit into a cloth sack, we traveled until we reached the town where my mother found work as a seamstress and eventually married my stepfather.

ALBERTUS

My mother, stepfather, and I live in a small gray house on the edge of town. There are three rooms in our house: downstairs, a kitchen and a room where my mother and stepfather sleep; upstairs, the attic, which is mine and which contains my bed, a bureau, and a box of my things. At one end of my attic is a small dusty window. The ceilings are low. I cannot walk upright, but it is my room and my stepfather never enters.

There is nothing exceptional about our lives. My mother gardens and makes clothes for small children during the day. My stepfather works in the glass factory. I go to school.

So far no one has questioned my human status. No one except my mother and me knows about my father. Not even my stepfather. He would not have married my mother had he known. When they met, my mother told him that my father had been killed in a fire. My stepfather did not ask for my papers. He is not much interested in me. But my mother made sure to tell him that my papers had been burned in the same fire that had killed my father.

"You had better get them duplicated before the boy goes to school," my stepfather replied.

The people of this town have known one another for a long time, and many are related by marriage. On holidays I see them gather in groups in the park, where they eat and drink. To them we are outsiders, strangers, as my stepfather also comes from a distant part of the country. We live quietly and do not disturb anyone, so we are tolerated.

My mother and stepfather sent me to the local school when I was seven. When they told me I was to go, I was in a panic. I could not touch my supper, nor could I sleep. My mother thought I was getting sick. I spent the next day in bed, where I tossed and turned anxiously while my mother sat in my room sewing a shirt for me to wear to school and talking to me in a low, quiet voice. Sometimes she sang to me—songs of the meadow that she sang when we lived with my father.

Toward the end of the afternoon we heard the school bells ring, and then the shouts of the children as they ran down the dirt roads.

"What is the matter?" my mother asked. "Why do you look so frightened?"

"What will I do about my papers when I go to school next week?" I said, burying my head in the pillow.

My mother touched my arm and said, "My poor child, I should have told you sooner. Your father has been very brave. He has left us something for you."

"My stepfather?" In two years he had never given me anything except a little gun he had carved on my birthday the year before.

"Your real father."

This was the first time my mother had spoken to me of him since we had left our home. "When was he here? Did you see him? What did he say?"

She shook her head. "No one saw him," she answered. "Not even I." She went out of the room. In a moment she was back, holding a silver sheet like the one she had shown the blue hunters. Thousands of tiny lines were etched on its surface and seemed to constantly change color and direction. "This is yours," she said.

For a moment I could not comprehend her words. How could I have papers? If this document told the truth, if it said that I was the son of an ox, I would be killed.

"Read it to me," I said to my mother.

The certificate was covered with hundreds of names thickly mapped. A living tree, gnarled and tangled, with deep roots. The names she read meant nothing to me. The only ones I recognized were hers and mine.

"Who are these people?"

"They are your ancestors."

My mother pointed to red seals in the center of the page and on all four corners.

"What do they say?"

"Certified Pureblood," my mother answered.

She pointed to a name linked with mine. The name was Albertus, and it was written in large curling letters.

"Who is he?"

"Your father."

"Is that his real name?" For I had never known my father's name.

She nodded.

"How did he get this?"

"I don't know," my mother said. "I found it one day under my laundry basket in the yard. It couldn't have been anyone but your father who put it there. No one else knows about you. And there were hoofprints in the yard. I covered them up, of course."

My father had come, and I hadn't even known! "Why didn't you tell me?"

"It is best not even to talk of your father." The back door slammed and we heard my stepfather's heavy tread. "We must never speak of him again."

My mother hurried downstairs, and I lay on my bed, studying the paper and its almost incomprehensible maze of names, thinking of my father.

How had he come by this paper? Who had put it together? How had he gotten his name stamped with the blood seals? And how had he even found us? He must have had friends—human friends, or animal friends of unusual ability—helping him. Then he was, perhaps, not lost and hungry, as I had often feared him to be.

And he was thinking of me, his half–human son.

I rolled the document carefully and tied it with a scrap of string. All night I slept with it in my hand, while the name Albertus sounded through my dreams.

PURE BLOOD OF THE HUMAN RACE

Every morning for five years my classmates and I have formed a large circle
around a mosaic of a man and a woman
standing in front of a fruit orchard with
the trees all in bloom. In blue and yellow
ribbons twined above their heads is written: FATHER ADAM, MOTHER EVE. PURE BLOOD
OF THE HUMAN RACE.

The teacher nods and we begin our daily
chant.

"We are human. We are nothing
but human.

"Our natures will never be degraded by contact with the animal world.

"Animals are a lower form of life.

"Animals stink. They are stupid. They have no souls.

"Animals and humans must never mix."

Then the teacher tells us the story we know so well by now: Once, a long time ago, men and women married animals. And from these pairings sprang all nature of evil—women with slashing talons and beaks, who killed human men; men who barked instead of talked and lapped up food with their tongues; children who crawled on the ground like snakes and hissed and bit their mothers. And even more unnatural: animals who recited poems and calculated the distance to the stars; animals who dared to set themselves up as the equals of men.

The teacher steps back and we recite: "But animals will never be the equals of man. And man must never descend to the level of animals."

We circle around the mosaic of Father Adam and Mother Eve. The sun bounces off the tiles and makes eyes gleam and lips shine and skin glint like hardened armor.

"The blue hunters with their shining swords will go into the forests, along the rivers, and among the crowds of cities. They will search out all tainted blood and destroy it.

"And we will be free, and pure, and cleansed."

At these words we fall to the floor, limp, as though released from a terrible hand.

"Pure blood of the human race!" we cry. And I think of my father, a mixed-blood ox. Has he found his brothers and sisters of the forest? Or has my father let some farmer yoke him to a plow for a few mouthfuls of moldy hay?

In school I am always afraid. The other students are so much quicker than I am. I am more at home in a grassy meadow than in a stifling classroom. Perhaps the others also dream of sky and sun, air and grass. I do not know.

My classmates mostly ignore me. Sometimes they make fun of my laugh. It is more like a snort, they say. I hear them call me Broadshoulder when they think I am not listening, and make jokes about my coarse hair and large feet and hands. When they pair us up to dance in circles, no one wants to be my partner. Still, the others don't dare to actively taunt me, because I am stronger than anyone in the class.

I cannot seem to learn from books. Numbers confuse me. I am lost on the great maps, with their cities, towns, and rivers. Only the velvety dark green of the forests attracts me. On the maps, forests shrink back from cities and towns. Surely this is a lie. It is the cities and towns that shrink at the approach of the forests.

We read every day about the stupidity of animals and the cleverness of men. I stumble over the words when it is my turn to read. The teacher tells me I am defiling the story, that I don't deserve to read it. Once when I was much younger, only seven, the teacher—angered by my slowness—called me a dumb ox. Some of the students smirked and grinned and pointed behind their hands.

The blood rose to my face. I felt exposed and so terrified that I wet my pants. The teacher stared at the dark stain running down my leg. Now, I thought, she will turn me in to the police. But instead she took me to the bathroom, cleaned me up, and hissed an apology. I was stupid, she said, exasperating, would try the patience of Mother Eve, but she shouldn't have called me an animal.

I often wonder if there are others like me. I once saw a little boy running down the street suddenly lift up and fly over a puddle, then land again on his feet and continue running as though nothing unusual had happened. In class I wonder if the little girl with her hair tied up in braids and the clean scrubbed face has an oriole for a grandmother. Or perhaps the boy who always wins first place at our games has wolf's blood running in his veins. Is our teacher first cousin to a cat? I think that a few of the others must hide invisible scales or fur or tails. Surely I cannot be the only one.

None will say, and I cannot tell. Perhaps it is for the best. If I cannot penetrate their secrets, they cannot penetrate mine.

I had one friend for a short time—a boy named Noah, whom I invited to my house. He was a sturdy boy, calm and happy, who had a talent for jumping and throwing a discus. Together Noah and I slid down haystacks, chased each other up and down the dirt road that runs behind our house, and picked wild berries and ate them until we were smeared with juice.

Sometimes when we had finished sliding and chasing and eating, we sat on a pile of stones in the middle of the meadow and talked. "Where do you think they live?" Noah asked one evening, pointing to the forest.

I knew that he spoke of the mixed animals.

"A secret lair?" I spoke as though I did not care where they lived, but my heart was pounding fast.

"The blue hunters would track it down," he said.

I thought of my father. "They must take refuge somewhere."

"The blue hunters would keep them on the run."

"Perhaps they have scouts to warn

them," I suggested. "The hunters have not yet destroyed them."

Noah shrugged. "Their numbers are dying every month, every day. That is what my father says."

I had seen Noah's father around town, a rough man with a loud voice. "He heard that in the pub," I said scornfully.

Noah gave me a searching look. I had said too much. Now he will turn on me, I thought. But instead he leaned close and spoke in my ear. "Sometimes I wish I might help them."

Long-hidden words and thoughts rushed forward. They seemed to choke me, so that I could not speak at all.

Noah jumped off the pile of stones we were sitting on. He looked frightened, and I knew that he had taken my silence for disapproval.

"You must never tell anyone," he pleaded. "Most of all my father."

I nodded, clambered down the rock pile, and the two of us began to make our way home in silence.

"Look!" cried Noah suddenly, pointing to the field we had just left.

I turned and saw a great white ox standing perfectly still in the dim blue twilight.

The animal was so beautiful . . . I ran to it and flung myself around its neck. The animal spoke quietly to me. "Do not put me or yourself in danger. Please go away."

It pushed me away and galloped toward the forest.

I walked back to my friend. Noah's face was pale and wondering. Now, I thought, we will speak openly. Instead he said, "You touched that bull."

"No," I said.

"I saw you!" He shoved me hard. "Smelly ox boy!"

I shoved him back. He punched me in the stomach, and I hurled myself at him. We rolled in the dusty road.

"Animal lover!" he shouted.

"You are too!" I retorted.

Noah picked himself up and ran down the road. We did not speak to each other ever again. But he never told anyone how I had embraced the ox. Nor did I betray his secret.

A FAMILY MEAL

Every night my stepfather sits on the front steps or in a chair by the fire and whittles with a small sharp knife from which little curls of fragrant wood erupt and fall. Once I reached out to gather them, but my stepfather put one heavy-booted foot down and stamped on the shavings.

He looks much like a wood carving himself. I think that his mother must have mated with a scrawny tree to have produced such a lackluster, awkward son.

After working all day at the glass factory, my stepfather doesn't want to move or talk, but when my mother comes in the room, he mutely follows her with his eyes. My mother is tall and slender, and my stepfather buys her rings and scarves and sometimes a bracelet or two. She puts them on when he is home, but when he has gone she takes them off and wears the plain dress she wore when we lived with my father.

My mother no longer sings all day as she once did. Still, from time to time a smile crosses her face, and I imagine that she is thinking of my father, somewhere deep in the forest.

One night my mother and I were sitting at the kitchen table peeling potatoes, when my stepfather entered. He was a little late, which was unusual.

"See what I have!" Proudly he held out a thick package of gray paper dripping with blood. "Meat. Freshly killed."

My mother froze, while I stared at the red blood seeping through the paper.

We never ate meat. No one did. Only the wealthiest had it occasionally. Meat had to be certified fit for human consumption—that is, one hundred percent animal—before anyone was allowed to eat it. That was a long and expensive undertaking.

"We'll have a good meal tonight!" said my stepfather. "It's good beef," he said. "Pureblood. Janney Peters showed me the papers. Haven't seen the likes of this in a long time. I paid a good amount for it, let me tell you."

This was the longest speech I had ever heard my stepfather make, but my mother made no move to take the meat.

"Well, what are you waiting for? Take it and cook it."

My mother touched the package with outstretched fingers.

I stood up. "I won't eat it."

"What?" my stepfather said. "Don't you know I paid half a week's wages for this meat?"

I reached into my pocket and clutched the pearly stones my father had given me long ago. "I won't eat it."

"You will."

I lowered my head. "I won't."

My stepfather's face darkened and his eyes darted from me to my mother. "You're . . ." he began. He seized my hand and opened my palm, searching it as though to find a clue to this unnatural resistance. I was holding one of the pearly stones.

"He still plays with these childish things," my stepfather said in disgust.

I did not answer, and he pushed me away. "The boy is not normal," he said.

My mother stood up. "I'll cook the meat," she said. "My son will eat it."

I watched her take down the big iron frying pan, and then I ran to my room.

But even there, in the attic with my door shut, the smell of burned flesh filled the room, entered my eyes and nose and mouth, until I ran to the window and tore it open and stood there taking great breaths of fresh cold air.

I heard a knock on my door, and my mother entered. "Come to the table."

"No," I began, but then stopped. Her voice was stern, but her eyes were frightened. I followed her downstairs and into the kitchen.

My stepfather was sitting expectantly in his carved wooden chair and did not look up as I slid into my seat. I watched my mother give him the largest piece of meat, then fill his plate with potatoes and greens. Then she put a small piece of meat on her own plate and an even smaller one on mine.

"Ah," said my stepfather with a sigh of contentment.

My mother forced a smile. I watched her pick at the food on her plate and finally put a morsel of meat into her mouth.

"Delicious," said my stepfather.

My mother nodded.

I nibbled at the potatoes and greens. It was hard to look at the meat, and the smell made me gag. Finally I pushed the plate away.

My stepfather glared at me. "What's the matter with this boy? He's not normal, I say!"

I dropped my fork and stood up. My stepfather also stood up. He raised his hand.

My mother had gone pale, but she said gently, "Please eat your food, both of you. It is very good."

My stepfather sank back into his chair.

I too sat down. I put a piece of meat into my mouth. And I thought, This is my *father*. My stomach rose up, my throat closed, I gagged.

My stepfather was watching me.

I tried again. I forced myself to chew the nauseating food once or twice. When my stepfather looked away, I spit it into my lap.

SUSEEN

I fell in love with a girl from my class. Her name was Suseen and she had glossy brown hair that hung in heavy curls down her back. I waited for her every day after school and followed her faithfully home. I didn't try to hide; I walked openly behind her. She and her friends would glance back at me and giggle.

After Suseen said good-bye to her friends and went into her house, I would linger in the road a while longer. Sometimes one or more small children would press their faces against a window to stare at me, but sometimes I caught a glimpse of Suseen walking from one room to the next. She lived in a much bigger house than ours. Her father ran a mill, and her cousins owned a large bakery.

Suseen was a good student, and in school when I stuttered over the day's reading, *The Wise Man and the Evil Snake* or *Tales of Ridicule,* the teacher often called on her to read the story as it should be read.

"He mangles the text as though he were wrestling with one of the Impure," the teacher said. The others would laugh, Suseen included. But sometimes as she picked up the book, Suseen would glance at me quickly, and I would see sympathy, not scorn, in her eyes.

★　　★　　★

One day the teacher told our class to bring our papers to school in three days. A special guest was coming—the police commissioner. He would examine our charts and award blood-purity certificates. The class would trace its human forebears as far back as possible, and the child with the longest lineage would win a prize.

The police commissioner was thin and dark-haired with moist, narrow eyes. "Does anyone have anything they want to tell me?" he asked as he stood at the front of the classroom.

We all looked nervously at one another.

"No?" He winked at us and his eyes gleamed knowingly. "Only pureblooded humans here, I see."

Perhaps he meant to put us at ease, but he only increased my terror. I looked down at my father's name, Albertus. Was there something in that name to identify him as a pureblood animal?

Would the commissioner sort through the maze of names and blood seals and find the ox hidden behind them?

I glanced at Suseen. Her certificate was rolled up with a piece of yellow yarn, and she was tapping it in a sleepy way against the edge of her desk.

The teacher clapped her hands, and the police commissioner moved to a chair at the side of the room.

Then we put on a play for him in which a swarm of blue-faced boys hunted down other children wearing animal heads. "Blue stands for strength," we recited. "Blue stands for thought. Blue stands for iron bands that encircle the enemy and keep them away from us."

I had the part of an honest goatherd trying to keep his flock together in the face of lions who quoted religious texts to my animals and urged them to flee to the forest. As part of my role, I brandished a club at the lions and pretended to strike them great blows, which were loudly cheered by the audience.

Later, the police commissioner sat at the teacher's desk and motioned to a boy in the first row to come forward. We all lined up after him to present our papers to the commissioner.

Even armed with the official silver certificate stamped with wax blood seals, I trembled to think that he would know that I was carrying a false document. At any moment he would pull out his black whistle, and the blue hunters would come and shoot me without a thought. But he merely glanced at my paper in a bored way and handed it back to me.

Much fuss was made over a flabby girl who ate candy all day long who was announced as the winner of the competition. She traced her human forebears back four hundred seventy-seven years—one hundred twenty-eight years more than anyone else in the class. The commissioner gave her a box of chocolates tied with a big blue ribbon.

Then we carried her triumphantly around the room in a chair held over our heads. As the strongest boy in the class, I had been selected as one of the carriers and could smell the chocolates that she constantly stuffed in her small pale mouth while we recited the sacred code: "We are human. We are nothing but human . . . Pure blood of the human race!"

That night, as I followed Suseen home, she and her friends were in high spirits. They tossed a ball from one side of the street to the other. Suseen threw it wild, and it shattered a window in Old Xerry the carpetmaker's house.

"Run!" I cried as he threw open the door.

I stood on the walk and watched Suseen and her friends disappear.

Old Xerry complained to my stepfather, and I had to work for him after school every day for a month. I rolled and unrolled carpets, swept, and carried water while Old Xerry worked his loom, muttering about irresponsible youth.

Once when he was sick, he sent for me on a Saturday. "Can I trust you, boy?" He raised himself up from his bed and pointed to a carpet that lay rolled up on the floor. "Take it to the grand house on the hill."

I heaved the carpet onto my shoulders and carried it across town. There an old woman directed me to lay it down in a back hallway. As I stood up to leave, I noticed that the floor was covered with green scales.

The woman looked sharply at me. "Xerry sent you?"

"Yes," I said.

She nodded as though reassured and sent me out the door with a handful of coins for the carpetmaker.

When I got back, Old Xerry snatched

the coins I gave him and counted them twice. Then he sank back on his pillow.

I waited to see if he needed something more from me.

"Here," Old Xerry said weakly. He pressed a coin into my hand. It was the first he had ever given me.

I took my coin and bought a small glass prism to lay on Suseen's desk the next school day.

LACEFLOWER

I was invited to Suseen's birthday party. Most of our class attended, as well as the teacher and all of Suseen's cousins. I was not used to parties, and I stood to one side while the others ran, jumped, and threw in games of skill. Suseen played in all the games, her glossy brown curls bouncing on her shoulders. I sat on the sidelines, sipped the too-sweet drink her mother had given me, and watched Suseen.

Then came the game where everyone took turns with bows and arrows in front of a large target that was covered by a picture of a deer with an evil look in its eye. Its front hoofs were firmly planted on a small dead child. Everyone shot at it until its entire body was pierced by arrows.

A bow and arrow were thrust at me. I fit the arrow into the bow with trembling hands. A lock of hair fell into my eyes and I awkwardly pushed it away. I pulled back the bow and let the arrow fly, hoping it would fall harmlessly into the grass. But my arrow flew straight to the target and pierced the heart of the deer.

My classmates cheered and handed me another arrow. As if it too had a will of its own, the second arrow found its way to the deer's heart. I bowed my head while the others shouted their approval.

Suseen took my arm. "You are too modest," she said. "No one else has made two hits in a row."

She led me to the table, which was covered with a fine rose-colored cloth, set with silver plates and cups, and crowned by a magnificent frosted cake made by her cousins the bakers.

The guests came running, the games forgotten.

As we left the party, Suseen handed each guest a small gift. The girls were given a necklace of blue and green stones. The boys received a wooden knife. When it came my turn to say good-bye, instead of the hard object I expected, Suseen pressed something light and fragile into my hand. I looked down. It was a tiny purple lace-flower.

From then on Suseen no longer joined in the laughter when the teacher made fun of my reading. When Suseen read in my place, she did so slowly and gravely, as though her words had a special power to somehow transform my mental dullness into her own brightness and quickness.

After she went into her house at the end of the day, Suseen now waved to me from her window.

The other girls teased her. "Your love," I heard them say. "Your handsome noble knight." When this happened, Suseen reddened and would turn away from me. But the next day she would bring me a small frosted cake at lunchtime.

One day a boy said, "Oh, Suseen leads him around by a ring in his nose!"

I became enraged and, lowering my head, charged the boy.

He screamed and fell, and the other boys came crowding around.

They brandished fists and sticks at me

and drove me off. "Animal!" they called after me. "Animal! Animal! Animal!"

I spotted Suseen and moved toward her, but she shrank back. I saw myself in her eyes: wild-eyed, disheveled, and streaked with blood and dust. "Suseen . . ." I said.

For a moment she seemed about to say something, but she turned away.

From that day on she refused to speak to me or even to look at me. I kept my distance and did not follow her home anymore.

THE RESCUE

After that, I went often to the forest. My stepfather did not like it, and it sometimes made my mother uneasy. But the forest was the only place where I felt at peace. I spent hours roaming among tangled trees, along silent streams, and through windy meadows. It was then that I felt close to my father.

I knew there was an invisible world that existed alongside my everyday world. I had heard about people fleeing to the forest and often hoped I would meet one of them. A schoolmate's cousin had disappeared last year, and it was said that he had gone to the forest. There were tales about flocks of birds with long red hair, round breasts, and shrunken, pale arms ending in talons. They were called motherbirds, and it was said that they stole small human children from their families and brought them to the forest to rear with mixed-blood animals.

In the forest I often fished. My stepfather liked fish, and when I brought some back, he was pleased and said that at least some good came out of my idle wanderings.

In school we had learned that fish were pure and safe—the only uncontaminated animals—but occasionally I found some that had to be thrown back. One had a dull green eye, just like the eye of the most popular girl in my class. The fish was long and silvery and much more beautiful than the girl was. Another one that I caught had long, flat beaverlike teeth. Still another had tiny perfect ears. When I saw these fish, I knew I should kill them.

Instead I put them in a pail and walked slowly up and down the bank of the stream. Then I tripped, knocking over the pail so the fish fell back into the water. I swore loudly and pretended to try and catch them again, in case anyone was watching.

One cold day my mother sent me to town to buy thread. I was returning home with my pockets full of colored spools when a man darted out a door. At first I thought he was wearing a special kind of suit, as he was clothed in soft brown fur from head to toe. Then I saw the pointed, twitching ears and the long furry neck. Fear radiated from his large eyes and quivering body.

From around the corner I heard shouts and the sound of heavy boots.

Running more swiftly and gracefully than anything I had ever seen, the deer-man bounded down the street.

Just then a familiar wagon came into sight. It was piled high with rugs, and Old Xerry was pushing it. He gave a low whistle, and to my astonishment the deer-man leaped onto the back of the wagon and crawled under the rugs.

Old Xerry's eyes met mine.

A moment later the blue hunters surged around the corner and surrounded the cart. "We're looking for something that's part deer and part man. Did you see it?"

"I'm just a poor carpetmaker with only

a stupid boy to help me—" Old Xerry whined.

"Spare us, old man. What's in your cart?"

"Only carpets!" croaked Old Xerry. "And I have to keep stopping to push them back on the cart because this lazy clumsy boy stacked them so poorly."

He gave me a shove and the blue hunters laughed. One of the hunters reached into the cart and yanked on one of the carpets.

I thought then that all the carpets would come tumbling out, and they would see the deerman huddled on the bottom of the cart, but the hunter only said, "There! I've straightened your pile."

"Thank you, sir," said Old Xerry. "I'm very much obliged."

"Let us know if you see it." They turned to leave. "Pure blood of the human race," they called.

"Pure blood of the human race," Old Xerry and I called after them.

Old Xerry took the handles of his cart, looked at me again, and then wheeled it rapidly away.

Now when I went to the forest, I thought of the deerman and wondered where Old Xerry had taken him. Was the deerman a friend of his? Or even a relative? I had many questions that I did not dare to ask him.

One day as I was picking berries at the edge of the forest, I heard shrill cries.

I dropped my pail and ran to a nearby creek, where an eagle with large human hands was choking a small wriggling animal.

"Help!" cried the animal. "Help me!"

I picked up a stick and drove the eagle off. It responded with a piercing shriek that made me drop to the ground and cover my head with my hands.

"*Die!*" screamed the eagle. "*Human waste!*"

It plucked a stone from the ground and hurled it at me. I ducked behind a tree. The eagle flew above me and grabbed for my head. I swung my stick at it again, and on a sudden inspiration I called out, "I have a gun!"

With a great flap of wings it soared away above the forest.

The eagle's prey lay in the shallows, half-covered with water. The creature was like nothing I had ever seen before. It looked like a cross between an otter and a centipede: short and plump and sleek, with a dozen slithery arms and legs that appeared entirely useless.

I picked it up. It was shaking with fear and cold. I put it under my shirt to warm it. Its eyes met mine—large, intelligent eyes, luminous almost—and there was an instant flash of communication between us.

"Thank you." Its voice sounded like a swift-running creek. "You saved my life."

"Where do you live?" I asked.

"My home and family have been destroyed. We lived in a stream not far from here, until the eagle diverted the course of the water and forced us out. I was the only survivor. Since then I have gone from puddle to pond searching for another place to live."

"You can come with me," I said. I picked up my pail of berries and set off through the forest with the otter under my shirt. Gradually his trembling subsided, and he fell asleep next to my chest. As for me, I was happy and content in a way that I hadn't been in a long time.

We were almost home when the forest became unnaturally still. The flowers closed up, the mushrooms shriveled, and the leaves on the trees turned silvery white and curled inward.

The otter awoke and shivered violently. "Hide!" he ordered in a shrill whisper.

I shoved the pail of berries under a bush and quickly climbed a nearby pine tree.

"What is it?" I whispered. He did not answer me, but I felt his heart beating and heard the quick intake of his breath.

Then I saw them, their blue faces, their

guns and heavy boots. They were carrying something wrapped in a burlap sack and laughing loudly.

"This one will get us a fine bounty," said one of the hunters.

"Look at those hands," said another. "That means double."

They dropped their sack to the ground, and the eagle fell out. Slapping the earth like a man, he pleaded, *"Do not kill me, good men."*

The men lifted their rifles.

I held the otter under my shirt as the shots rang out. His smooth warm body trembled violently against mine. I sat hunched on a tree limb, not daring to move or even to breathe.

They cut off the head and one hand of the eagle and lit a pyre around its remains. Then the hunters stood in a circle and recited, "We are human. We are nothing but human . . ."

They left with their bounty in the burlap sack.

"Yours is not a kind race," said the otter.

"I am not one of them."

The otter studied me. "You look like a human. How are you not one of them?"

"I am the son of an ox." I had never before spoken those words aloud. They sounded strange to my ears and seemed to echo all through the forest.

The otter said nothing, but I saw compassion in his eyes.

The shouts and songs of the blue hunters gradually disappeared from the forest. I climbed down slowly from the tree, and we set off for home.

THE OTTER'S TALES

The otter slept with me at night, curled in the curve of my legs. And while I was at school, he stayed under my bed in a basin of cool water.

Each day I brought fish to him, fresh fish that I caught in the creek at the edge of the forest.

When my stepfather was home, he always wanted to know what I caught, and where, and how many, and was it easy. Did I see any that should be reported? Under his watchful eye I had to empty my pail outside and gut and clean the fish.

Then I brought the fish to my mother in the kitchen. "Leave them on the table," she said. I spread the fish out on a sheet of heavy paper and slipped one or two into my pocket. My mother always seemed to have her back turned, though once I caught her eye in the reflection from the window. Her expression did not change, nor did she say anything.

One day I tiptoed upstairs to surprise the otter and found my mother singing softly to him. I stopped on the stairs and silently watched them. She cradled the otter in her arms and hummed a tune I knew from long ago. I slipped back down the stairs. The otter never spoke of my mother. Nor did my mother speak of the otter to me.

Several times I took the otter out to the creek. I put him in a basket and covered him with grass and twigs. We had long happy afternoons splashing in the creek, and when we were ready to come home, I covered him with piles of small wormy apples.

One night my stepfather was waiting for me on the front steps with his wood and his knife.

He pointed at the apples with his knife. "What do you need those for?"

"The worms," I answered. "We study them in school." My heart was beating fast, and I hoped he did not notice how flushed I was.

"You study vile animals?"

"Only to demonstrate our superiority," I answered quickly.

"Well, go in! What are you standing there for?" he said.

My stepfather was suspicious. I worried. What if he came home unexpectedly from the glass factory? I told the otter that he must never speak when my stepfather was in the house, even in his sleep. If he was discovered, he must never let on that he understood the speech of humans.

Of course he knew this far better than I did.

The otter told me many wonderful tales. He understood the language of stones and stars and moss and roses. Of water dripping in dark caves. Of sand flying in the wind. Of tightly wrapped leaves bursting from buds.

Like my mother, he too told me of the time when animals and humans began to communicate—when they no longer held each other in fear and contempt.

"When humans and animals began to marry," the otter told me in his low, deep, water voice, "some animals became miraculously intelligent. They attacked problems and mysteries with a ferocity, an unswerving concentration, and it seemed as though they could ferret out the secrets of the universe.

"As for humans, their instincts were enhanced. They became powerful musicians whom no one could resist, magnetic lovers, charismatic leaders, mysterious preachers.

"Sometimes, however, the animal nature seemed to paralyze the human being with shame. A feathered man hid in his house, ashamed to be seen by either friend or family. A girl with an eagle's beak and piercing eyes wore a veil over her face and never married. A man whose arms, legs, and chest were covered with shining silver scales went from one doctor to another claiming he had a mysterious disease and demanding a cure, when everyone knew that his mother was a snake."

Another time he said, "When human nature was added to the animal, the animals were given the opportunity to express deep, untouched springs in their nature. A following grew up around a dog who was said to have found peace and freedom while contemplating nature by a pure spring. He was a great handsome dog, shaggy and eloquent, with gentle eyes and an air of complete stillness. He made his home in the forest, where many of the new breed of creatures joined him, as well as some pure humans and animals."

I lay on my back pondering these wonders and staring at the dark rafters while the moon poured through my dusty window.

"There are those who say that the dog still lives in the deepest forest," said my friend. "No hunter could ever find him. It was in this time that the blue hunters arose and began to hunt those with mixed blood."

"The teachers say that almost all the Impure are dead," I said to the otter. "But we are alive, and I have seen others."

"Yes," said the otter. "There are many others."

DISCOVERY

This is how we were discovered.

It was a hot summer day, and I had taken the otter out for a swim. I didn't take him out very often anymore—it was too hard to get him back into the house. My stepfather was more and more suspicious of me. He sometimes searched my knapsack when I had spent the day in the forest and made me empty my pockets.

Once I had to leave the otter in a field until my stepfather was out of the way. I put the otter in a small pool of water surrounded by tall grasses. "Come back soon," the otter said. His large, glittering eyes were full of fear.

I too was afraid—my mind was filled with thoughts of blue hunters, predatory birds, and prowling forest cats. I waited until my stepfather was asleep, and then I crept out of the house in the dark. The nighttime landscape was unfamiliar and confusing, and it took me a long time to find the otter. When I finally reached him, he was shivering and mute. I bundled him in a sack and carried him home.

"I have lost the knack of living alone in the wild," he told me. "You must never leave me."

"I will not," I promised.

We did not have any outings for a long time after that.

That hot day when we were discovered, my stepfather had announced at breakfast that he would be gone until late that night. I ran upstairs to tell the good news to the otter.

When my stepfather had gone, I put the otter in a sack and we set off for the stream. There I freed the otter into the water, left my clothes in a pile on the bank, and jumped into the stream. The otter swam ahead and teased me, calling me a slow-poke.

We played in the stream for a while, then drifted sleepily on our backs, looking up at the sky and its towering white clouds. The overhanging trees created patches of light and shadow that moved over our faces.

"Did you know the animals once had names?" began the otter. His voice sounded like the rippling notes of the stream.

"When my father sent my papers, I saw his name for the first time."

"Yes," said the otter. "In earlier times, before the blue hunters, all the mixed-blood were stripped of their names. Some secretly kept their names, however, and passed them on to their children."

"Do you have a name?" I asked.

The otter paused. "We only tell our names to our family, and sometimes to a very close friend. Since you are my very dear friend, I will tell you mine."

I heard the crackle of twigs and small plants being trampled underfoot but dismissed it as a wild cow searching for food.

"My name is Theodore," he said.

"Theodore," I echoed.

The next moment we were surrounded by hunters, their faces painted blue, guns

cradled in their arms. The otter dived under the water, but the hunters raised their
guns and fired.

I screamed.

They pointed their rifles at me. The
stream was red with Theodore's blood.
Now I am going to die, I thought.

"Get out!" one of the men ordered me
roughly. *"Out!"* he shouted. "Or we
shoot!"

I climbed out of the stream and stood
shivering in front of the hunters. One of
them threw me my shirt and pants. Perhaps they would not shoot me after all, I
thought, if they wanted me to get dressed.

Another of the blue-faced men came
forward. "You stupid boy," he said.

I recognized my stepfather's voice.

He jerked me forward.

"He has committed a very serious crime," said one of the hunters. "Consorting with a mixed-blood animal."

"He is stupid," my stepfather replied. "He doesn't know what he is doing."

"Say you're sorry," he whispered.

I did not speak.

My stepfather dug his fingers into my arms.

"My stepson is not very smart," he said loudly to the other men. "Say you didn't mean it!" he hissed at me. "Say that animal enchanted you and led you astray!"

I stared silently at him.

"Little fool!" he growled. "I'd just as soon let you die. It's your mother I'm thinking of."

I still did not answer, but turned my head stubbornly away.

One of the hunters stepped closer. "He

must be punished for his crime. Give him to us."

"I'll take care of him." My stepfather slapped me again and again. Then he took me by the throat and began to choke me.

Then my father's nature—that slow, persistent, steady, and volcanic nature—reasserted itself. I loosened my stepfather's fingers from my neck, picked him up, and hurled him into the bloody stream.

PRISON

They put me in a cell with a pallet of straw and a trough of water. The guards were supposed to come twice a day to bring me food and water. One was especially cruel. Instead of food he sometimes shoved heaps of rotting hay through my door. "Here, animal lover," he would say.

I often heard him with another man outside my cell. They laughed and talked in great detail of the animals they had killed and how they had died. The guard would always conclude with the words, "And that in there is no better than an animal. When he gets out, we'll shoot him down and collect a bounty on his head."

One day he was changing the straw on the pallet when his shirt fell open and I saw his feathered chest.

He caught my stare and hastily closed his shirt.

"Do not worry. I will not reveal your secret," I said.

Gathering up the dirty straw, he ran from the cell.

Soon after, that guard disappeared. He was afraid of me, I think. Perhaps he left town or found another job before I could betray him. Or had another person glimpsed his feathered chest and reported him? If that was so, perhaps he, like Theodore, was dead now.

The guard who took his place did not have the animosity of the first. My water was changed regularly and I received my meals on time.

After a month, they brought me to trial. The courtroom was like a school, with wooden benches and a map on the front wall. The judge, a big man with the dull look of one who eats too much meat, looked at me without interest and called the witnesses to testify.

They stood their rifles against the benches in an orderly row and walked heavily to the front of the room. They had painted their faces blue for this day. While I sat to the left of the judge with a guard on either side of my chair, the blue hunters told of how they had heard the animal and the boy laughing and talking together in full violation of written and unwritten human law. Of how they had crept up to the stream and surprised us. Of how they had done their duty and instantly shot the animal.

They told the court that they had waded into the stream and taken the body of the otter. They had cut off one leg for the bounty and then hung the otter on a pole and left it in the forest as a warning to any other animal that might think of corrupting a human boy.

Then came my stepfather, who told the judge that he had not expected to find me in the stream with the otter. But it had not surprised him. I was a stubborn, difficult boy, who would not take direction from his elders and betters. But I was young and perhaps not completely hopeless. My mother was a gentle, sensible woman. With the proper training I might yet be salvaged . . .

The judge dismissed the hunters and called me to him. He made me kneel by his desk. Then he spoke in a low voice. "You know the penalty for consorting with an animal."

I nodded.

"You are lucky that the hunters did not shoot you along with the animal," he said sternly.

I said nothing.

"It would have been no more than you deserved," he added. "It is your stepfather whom you must thank for saving your life." Then he slapped me lightly on the face and told me to get to my feet. "You may still die. Think on it."

The two guards gripped my arms and led me back to the cell.

Because of my youth, they did not execute me. Instead I was sentenced to hard labor and forbidden to speak to other humans.

"You have harbored an animal and you will be treated like one," said the judge when he sentenced me.

They yoked me to a plow and had me till the fields. I carried stone to build walls, I dug wells and pulled carts of timber.

There were five other prisoners who labored alongside me. They had committed crimes against men, such as thievery, fraud, or abuse, and their work was much lighter. To them fell the planting of seeds, the scything of long grasses, the burning of brushwood. Of course they did not speak to me or even acknowledge that I was there.

I did not mind the hard labor—I was strong and young and it was in my blood to work the fields. I did not mind the hostile stares of my fellow prisoners as long as I was working the earth under the sky.

Then after many months I was again confined to a cell, a dark room that had only one small window that was set near the ceiling.

"You enjoyed it too much outside," said one of the guards who escorted me to my new cell. "Now you'll see what prison is really like."

A feeble gleam of sun passed high across my walls in the early morning, and then the room was gray until the next morning. I would stretch out my hands to bathe them in the weak rays of sunlight. Sometimes, desperate to feel light and warmth on my face, I would jump again and again toward the window.

My mother was not allowed to visit me. Indeed, I never received any letters from her. She would not abandon me, I thought. Perhaps my stepfather had forbidden her to write, or perhaps the guards destroyed her letters before they got to me.

Once a note came through the window. It was a piece of rough paper with a lace-flower pinned to it. There were no words, only a tiny *s* in one corner.

The flower soon wilted, but I propped it against the wall so it caught my eye throughout the day.

My only companions were the ants that scuttled along the floor. They were not intelligent like my friend Theodore, but I took pleasure in their movement and in their constant search for food. I often crumbled a bit of bread in one corner of the cell and watched them swarm over it.

The otter had told me many stories about animals repaying the kindness of humans and about humans who were indebted to animals. I wondered if these ants wished to help me in any way. Perhaps they could bring me a key to unlock the door of my cell or lead me to a tunnel out of the prison. If they all worked together, the ants might wear down the stone of that high window, and light and air would flood my cell.

But the ants did nothing to release me from the dark cell. And the weeks lengthened to months, and my labor in the fields now seemed like a distant paradise.

TO THE FOREST

They released me from jail after a year. When my stepfather brought me home, a crowd of people had gathered around our house. I was dazzled by the light and the vast sky, and at first I thought that they had come to greet me.

Then I heard the threatening murmurs. My stepfather gripped my arm and pushed me through the crowd. I saw two of Suseen's baker cousins talking intently to a gaunt woman with large bulging eyes. I wondered if Suseen was somewhere nearby.

When we got to the house, my step-father banged his fist three times on the door. It opened abruptly, and we stumbled in. Then it slammed shut behind us.

My mother and I embraced. "You have grown thin," she said. "And much taller."

She looked tired and sadder, but I did not tell her this.

The crowd outside stayed and began to chant, "Pure blood of the human race." My mother drew the curtains.

All day I stood near the window at the back of the room, where I could see the sky and the fields.

Every evening people stood in front of our house shouting and chanting. But in time their numbers dwindled, and finally they came no more.

One day I left the house and went to

the stream. I found no trace of the otter. Even the stick where the blue hunters had hung him was gone.

The days passed. I did a few odd jobs for Old Xerry. But he had little work and no one else would hire me.

I went into town. It was the middle of the afternoon and the streets were deserted. I saw Suseen in her cousin's bakery, where she now worked. She wore a white apron over a green dress, and her hair was pinned up with a comb. Her hands, dusted with flour, deftly sliced peaches into a pastry dish.

When she saw me, she stopped her work. "You're back," she said.

We stood there a moment. Then her cousin entered with a tray of pastries on his shoulder.

Suseen pushed a bread across the counter at me.

I fished in my pocket for some coins and left quickly.

My stepfather told me he was ashamed to live in the same house as me. If it was up to him alone, he would have sent me out into the streets long ago. Only because of my mother had he let me stay. Now I must leave.

He washed his hands of me.

I saw myself going from town to town in search of work, and the bleak friendless days of my future stretched out in front of me.

I did not know what to do, and when I went to my mother, she said only one word. "Wait."

Then she called me to her. She was in

the yard, a basket of freshly washed laundry at her feet. My stepfather's work shirts hung stiffly on the line.

"Look." My mother pointed to a patch of bare earth almost concealed by tall grasses where I saw the fresh hoofprints of an ox.

"He has come for you," she said.

The next day just before dawn my mother woke me. My stepfather was still asleep when we left the house. She gave me a knapsack of food, which I hoisted over my shoulder. The air was cool and soft as we walked along the dirt road that led to the forest.

We crossed the field where Noah and I had played so long ago. And from the shadows of the forest a great brown ox emerged.

"My son," he said.

I grasped his horns and climbed onto his back.

"Are you comfortable, my son?"

"Yes, Father."

My mother reached into her pocket, pulled out the blue velvet sack with the pearly stones, and hung it around my neck. Then for a moment she leaned her cheek against my father's head.

The sun came over the trees, and my father and I plunged into the forest.

At times my father carries me on his back, and at times I walk alongside him. Each night I gather wood and make a fire to cook with and keep us warm. We travel over pathless roads searching for the lost animals, my half-brothers and half-sisters.

When we meet them, we share our food and our fire. There is great rejoicing. To them I am neither a human boy nor an animal. I am the oxboy.

ANNE MAZER grew up in a family of writers in Syracuse, New York. Originally intending to be an artist, she studied at the School of Visual and Performing Arts at Syracuse University. She then went to the Sorbonne, in Paris, where she studied French literature. She is the author of *Moose Street*, a middle-grade novel, and three picture books: *Watch Me*, illustrated by Stacey Schuett; *The Yellow Button*, illustrated by Judy Pedersen; and *The Salamander Room*, illustrated by Steve Johnson. *The Oxboy* was inspired by a poem she wrote.

Ms. Mazer lives with her husband and two children in northern Pennsylvania.